Watch out for the ~~w~~

The cottage door flew ~~...~~ ~~...~~ *hedgehog ran outside dragging a big, thick book. "Delay her!" they cried. Stumbling and panting, they disappeared into the wood.*

Just in time! There came the witch shuffling nearer with a basket full of leafy plants on her arm. Without looking up, she shuffled into the cottage and slammed the door shut behind her.

The owl hid behind a large tree. He waited, his heart beating. When would she notice?

"Oohoo oohoo oohoo!" A piercing noise came suddenly from inside the cottage. "My book of magic! Thieves! Burglars! Oohoo oohoo oohoo!"

OTHER PUFFIN BOOKS YOU MAY ENJOY

TALES
OF THE
WICKED
WITCH

Hanna Kraan

Illustrations by
Annemarie van Haeringen

Translated by
Elisabeth Koolschijn

PUFFIN BOOKS

PUFFIN BOOKS

Published by the Penguin Group

Penguin Putnam Inc., 375 Hudson Street, New York, New York 10014, U.S.A.

Penguin Books Ltd, 27 Wrights Lane, London W8 5TZ, England

Penguin Books Australia Ltd, Ringwood, Victoria, Australia

Penguin Books Canada Ltd, 10 Alcorn Avenue, Toronto, Ontario, Canada M4V 3B2

Penguin Books (N.Z.) Ltd, 182-190 Wairau Road, Auckland 10, New Zealand

Penguin Books Ltd, Registered Offices: Harmondsworth, Middlesex, England

First published in the United States of America by Front Street, 1995
Published in Puffin Books, 1997

1 3 5 7 9 10 8 6 4 2

LIBRARY OF CONGRESS CATALOGING-IN-PUBLICATION DATA
Kraan, Hanna.
[Verhalen vande boze heks. English]
Tales of the wicked witch / Hanna Kraan : illustrated by Annemarie Haeringen ;
translated by Elisabeth Koolschijn.
p. cm.
"Originally published in the Netherlands under the title Verhalen
van de boze heks"—verso t.p.
Summary: Consists of fourteen episodes in the lives of forest
animals and their resident witch, whose cauldron, much to
her dismay, contains more fun than nastiness.
ISBN 0-14-038336-0 (pbk.)
[1. Witches—Fiction. 2. Forest animals—Fiction.]
I. Koolschijn, Elisabeth. II. Haeringen, Annemarie van, ill.
III. Title.
PZ7.K857Tal 1997 97-13628 CIP AC

Printed in the United States of America

TABLE OF CONTENTS

THE WICKED WITCH IS FURIOUS

A strange noise sounded through the wood. From a distance you might have thought it was an autumn storm, but it was not that. It was the wicked witch, who was running through the wood ranting and raging.

"Oo, I'm so angry!" she cried. "Oohoo oohoo oohoo, I'm so terribly angry! How dare you laugh, squirrel? There, now you've got something to laugh about." She waved her magic wand, and *whoosh!*—a pine cone lay where the squirrel had been sitting. "That's that," screeched the witch. "Anyone else interested? Perhaps you toadstools?" and *whoosh!*—a few pebbles now lay where the toadstools had been standing. Stamping her feet, the witch hurried on, and along her way she turned snails into twigs, blueberries into blackberries, blackberries into blueberries, and an old toad into a molehill.

The animals had hidden as far away as possible and were waiting anxiously for the witch to stop raging. But that was taking a very long time.

"We must do something," said the hare, who had crawled into a deep hole with a few other animals. "If she goes on like this much longer, she will have changed the whole wood with her witchcraft. And we have to live here, after all."

The animals nodded gravely, but what they should do, nobody knew.

"We could attack her," cried a beetle.

The hare shook his head. "Much too dangerous," he said.

"We should talk to her," said the owl. "Just talk calmly, then her bad mood will wear off."

"A marvelous idea," sneered the blackbird. "You'll do that, I suppose?"

"Me?" asked the owl, shocked. "Well no, I'd prefer to stay alive and well."

"I'm not going either," cried another animal. "I wouldn't do it for anything, not me."

"Hmm . . . ," said the hare.

Then someone yawned right at the back of the hole and a sleepy voice said, "I'll go and have a chat with her."

The animals looked up, surprised. There they saw the bat, who was stretching.

"Let me go," said the bat. "I'm not afraid of that showoff."

And while the animals moved aside respectfully, he dropped down and swooped out of the hole in search of the witch.

He did not have to search for long. Rumbling footsteps resounded, and there was her shrill voice: "Oohoo oohoo oohoo, I'm so peeved, I'm furious! Hopping mad! Ugh!"

"Witch!" cried the bat. "Witchy!"

"Watch out, bat," groaned the witch. "I don't dislike you, but I'm so angry I might cause you mischief."

"Why are you so angry?" asked the bat.

"Why?" cried the witch. "I'll tell you why! I'm so angry because that—that—er . . . wait a minute, I . . . What's this? I've forgotten, how odd!"

And the witch flopped down onto a treetrunk

and started to think carefully.

"If you don't know why you're angry any-more, then it's worn off," said the bat.

"Yes," said the witch, surprised. "It's worn off. Well then, I'll go home." She got up and shuffled in the direction of her cottage.

"Wait a minute," the bat called after her. "Aren't you going to turn everything back again with your witchcraft?"

"Oh yes, it's a good thing you said that." The witch waved her magic wand lazily.

Whoosh! Whoosh! Whoosh! There. The mole-hill became a toad again, the blueberries became blackberries and the blackberries became blueberries, the twigs became snails again, the pebbles became toadstools again, and the pine cone became a squirrel again.

"All right now?" asked the witch, and when the bat nodded, she shuffled on. "Oh my, how tired I am," the bat heard her mumbling.

The bat turned round and fluttered back to the hole. "It's been taken care of," he said. "You can go home."

"Hooray!" cried the animals.

"Well done," said the hare.

"Thank you," said the owl.

And off they went.

Contentedly, the bat watched them go. He yawned, stretched, and said, "There we are, now at least I can go back to sleep!"

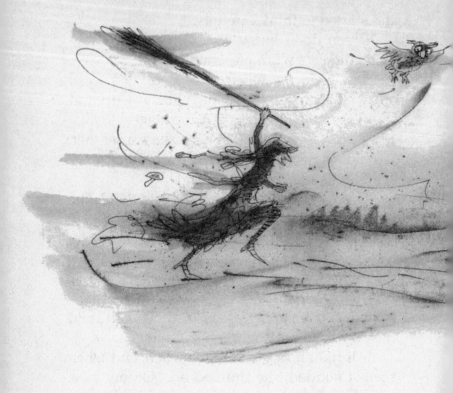

THE WICKED WITCH MUST GO

The wicked witch was at it again! Waving her broomstick, she ran after all the animals she came across.

"Oohoo oohoo oohoo!" screeched the witch. "I'll get you! Oohoo oohoo oohoo!"

Most of the animals had taken cover at the sandbank and were waiting anxiously until the

danger had passed. They could not see the witch from there, but they could hear her.

"Oohoo oohoo oohoo!" The sound was shrill. "Pests! I'll get you!"

At last, after what seemed a long time, the raging died down and ended completely when the witch slammed her cottage door with a bang.

The hare got up with some difficulty. He brushed sand off his fur and said, "This can't go on any longer. This is her third fit of anger this week. We're not safe here."

"Either she chases us through the entire wood or she casts the maddest magic spells," muttered the fox.

"Yes," complained the rabbit. "The other day, she turned my uncle into a bluebottle fly. We were scared to death when he came home. It wasn't until days later that she turned him back again."

"And she tied knots in my spines!" cried the hedgehog.

Now the stories began. Everyone had experienced a frightening adventure at the hands of the witch at some time or another.

"In short," said the hare, "enough is enough.

And because it's impossible trying to talk to her, she'll have to leave here. Go away."

The animals nodded. "But how do you think you'll manage that?"

The hare looked round the circle cunningly.

"While you were all just lying there thinking about yourselves, I thought of a plan. Listen." And whispering, he went on: "She has a sister who lives in the south. Tomorrow we'll go to her . . ."

"To her sister?" asked the hedgehog.

"No! To the witch. And we'll say that her sister has asked if she'll go down to the south immediately. Then we'll be rid of her for the time being. Who knows, she might stay there for good."

"Will she fall for that?" asked the hedgehog. "I'll believe it when I see it."

But the next day, when the witch heard that her sister needed her, she immediately took her broomstick and flew south.

"There, we're rid of her," said the hare.

Life in the wood had become quite different now. No screeching, no wild chases, everything was calm.

A few weeks later, everything was still calm. Indeed, it seemed as if the animals were becoming quieter and quieter . . .

One evening, when they were all sitting

together lazily in the autumn sun, the hedgehog said suddenly, "I wonder how the wicked witch is doing."

"Why should you care?" said the hare with a yawn. "She's gone, and we have peace and quiet."

"Peace and quiet, yes," said the hedgehog. "You could safely say that it's a dull old place here since she's gone. It may sound strange, but I miss that woman."

The animals looked at one another. Then the fox said, "Now that you mention it, it's been very boring recently. The excitement has gone."

"But . . ." said the hare.

"Yes!" cried the animals. "The witch must come back! The witch must come back!"

"We're all getting too fat now that we don't have to run away from her anymore," said the hedgehog.

"But . . . ," said the hare. Then he saw two rabbits with a banner: WHERE IS OUR WITCH? "Well now," he said. "It's all right with me. To be honest, I've been thinking about it as well."

The animals decided to send a message with the migratory birds. They all flew south at this time anyway; they could easily ask the witch if she would come back.

Now there was nothing to do but wait.

Every day the animals looked up at the sky impatiently. Where was she?

At last, on a bleak, gray afternoon, they saw a familiar figure, high in the sky on a broomstick. There she was again!

When the witch landed in a clearing in the wood, everyone was waiting for her. A choir of rabbits sang, "Welcome, welcome to our wood," and the cuckoo presented flowers.

"Ah, the witch!" cried the others together. "Had a good journey? What was it like in the south?"

The witch, greatly touched, blew her nose.

The buzz of voices went on until the hare pointedly cleared his throat a few times.

"Shh, shh!" cried the hedgehog.

"Witch," said the hare in a solemn tone, "we are truly sorry that a few weeks ago we enticed you away with an excuse and we're very happy that—"

"*What!*" screamed the witch. "Enticed me away! Well, well! That's why my sister knew nothing about it. An excuse! I'll get you! Oohoo oohoo oohoo!" And she ran toward the hare. Rustle, rustle, all the animals had gone. Giggling and pushing, they were heading for the sandbank.

"Hooray, everything's back to normal," cried the hare. "Run for it, folks!"

CHRISTMAS IN THE WOOD

Far into the wood, past the pool and then to the left, there stands a huge pine tree. In front of the tree there is a clearing. It is always absolutely silent here. The animals hardly ever come, and even the wicked witch rarely shows her face in this part of the wood. But on the afternoon before Christmas, cracking and rustling could be heard near the tree. The hare and the hedgehog appeared.

"I mean this clearing," said the hare. "Just right for our Christmas party. There's a pine tree, there's enough room for all the animals, and it's far away from the wicked witch's cottage."

The hedgehog shuddered. "Don't talk about the witch," he said. "Last week, she put knots in my spines again. If I even think about it . . ."

"Yes, yes, yes," said the hare. "She's simply not to be trusted. But if you think this is a good spot as well, then we'll tell the others that they're to come here. And I'll ask the spiders and the squirrels if they'll decorate the tree."

As dusk began to fall, all the animals came to the clearing and sat down in a large circle. When everyone was sitting, the hare said, "Come on, we're going to sing a Christmas carol."

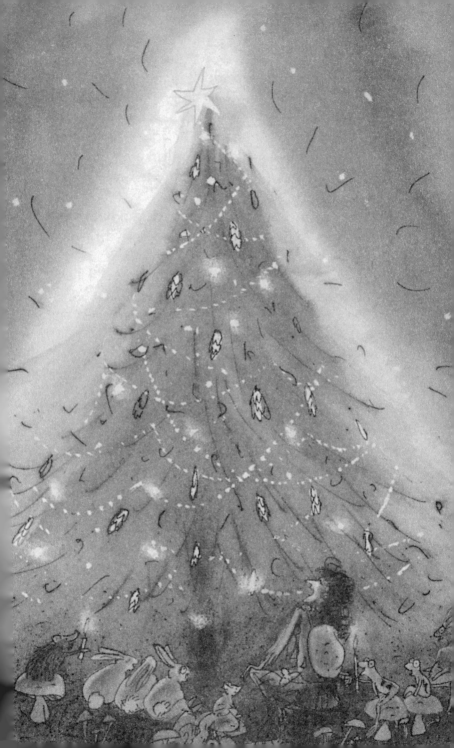

The carol resounded through the quiet wood, and while they sang, the animals all looked at the huge pine tree. It was beautifully decorated with nuts and pine cones, the spiders had spun threads that looked like angels' hair, and hundreds of fireflies provided a soft light that beamed from the tree.

When the carol was finished, the hare said, satisfied, "This is really Christmas, with everyone together . . ."

"Still, I miss someone," said the owl. "Hasn't the witch been invited?"

An embarrassing silence fell, and everyone looked at the hare.

The hare cleared his throat. "No," he said, "I preferred not to have her here. She is capable of ruining the whole party with her witchcraft. And that mood of hers—save me from that."

"You're right," cheeped the titmouse. "She almost caught me yesterday. I don't even want to think about it!"

"She put knots in my spines last week!" cried the hedgehog.

"And she put my . . . ," began the magpie.

The owl nodded. "I know she's no angel. But it *is* Christmas."

The hare shrugged his shoulders. "Go and get her then if you dare. Well, what are you waiting for with all your big talk?"

The owl got up. "You can say all sorts of

things about me," he said in a dignified manner, "but I'm no coward. I'm going. See you later . . . or not, of course," he added more softly and stiffly as he spread out his wings.

"We'll never see him again," whispered the hedgehog. "That creature is capable of anything. Last week she put knots in—"

"Yes, but be quiet now!" snarled the hare nervously. "We should never have let him go."

The animals waited dejectedly.

In the meantime, the owl flew to the witch's cottage. He circled the roof a few times, landed in front of the window, hesitated for a minute, and tapped carefully on the cracked pane.

There was a bumping sound and the slovenly figure of the witch appeared behind the window. "What do you want?" she screeched.

"Merry Christmas," said the owl. "We're singing carols around the huge pine tree, and on behalf of all the animals I've come to invite you."

Astounded, the witch looked at him "On behalf of all the animals," she repeated. And then: "Do they want me to join them?"

"Yes, certainly," said the owl, "as I said—" But he did not get any further.

"Well!" screeched the witch. "And how do I know it isn't a trap? How do I know that? You and your carols. I'm not going to fall for that!"

"But listen a minute," began the owl.

"Listen! I'm not going to listen! Go away before I lose my patience! Well, aren't you going to get a move on?"

The owl had no alternative. He turned and flew slowly away.

At the clearing, the animals heaved a sigh of relief when they saw the owl again above the treetops.

"What did she say? Tell us!" they cried.

The owl sat down. "I did my best," he said, disheartened, "but she didn't trust us. I still think it's a shame."

"Well, I don't!" cackled the hedgehog. "Last week she even put knots in my spines . . ." He caught his breath and looked at the bushes, his eyes bulging. "There she is!" he said in a shrill voice.

The animals looked up, frightened. Yes, there stood the witch, leaning on her broomstick. She looked slowly around the circle; then the pine tree, which was shining softly outlined against the dark sky, caught her eye. For a long time she said nothing. Then she sighed and whispered, "How beautiful . . ." And then aloud: "There should be something on top, really."

Whoosh! A bright light beamed on top of the tree.

The witch nodded and said shyly, "I'll be off

again now," and she got ready to leave.

The hare, who like the others had been watching speechlessly, jumped up. "Don't go!" he cried. "Stop, stop, you belong here too!" He ran to the witch, grabbed her arm, and pulled her to the circle. "Move up a bit, all of you," he said. "You sit down."

The witch sat down hesitantly.

"The next carol," said the hare.

The animals began to sing, and the witch sang with them softly. But when she saw that the animals were nodding at her encouragingly, she began to sing louder and louder. Before long, she was singing the loudest of them all.

In between carols, the witch felt someone pulling hard on her sleeve. It was the hedgehog.

"Nothing in particular," said the hedgehog, "but last week . . ."

Suddenly he smiled and said, "Oh, never mind. Merry Christmas!"

NEW YEAR'S RESOLUTIONS

It was the beginning of January. The hare sat in front of his house with a plate of doughnuts. He picked up a doughnut, sighed, and reluctantly took a bite.

The hedgehog came walking along the path.

He looked sleepily at the plate. "Is that your breakfast?"

The hare nodded and with his mouth full said, "Have one too."

The hedgehog shuddered. "No, thank you. I don't want to see a doughnut again before next New Year's Eve."

"They've got to be eaten up," said the hare.

The hedgehog sat down next to him and yawned.

The hare took another doughnut and asked, "Have you made any New Year's resolutions this year?"

"New Year's resolutions? Me? No, of course not, I never do."

"I do!" said the hare. "I always make a whole list. To visit lonely animals more often, to be less impatient, to be helpful, and that sort of thing."

"And what does it all come to?" asked the hedgehog scornfully. "Next week you'll have forgotten all about it."

"No, I won't have. Really. All right, it doesn't always come to much, but at least I try."

"Rubbish," said the hedgehog. "Nonsense. I always say—"

But the hare never got to know what he always said, because just at that moment a large net was thrown over the two animals and they could hear shrill laughter: "Hi hi, ha ha!"

"Help!" squeaked the hedgehog, and the

hare nearly choked himself with shock.

"Hi hi, ha ha! Two at once under one net. Only a wicked witch could do that!"

The hare and the hedgehog tried to crawl out from under the net, but they did not succeed. The net was secured by a magic spell. They had been caught.

"Hi hi, ha ha!" jeered the witch, and she danced round the net.

The hedgehog looked at her angrily. "Stop all that screaming and jumping. I've just gotten up. And take that dirty fishnet away."

"I wouldn't dream of it. You're going to stay right here. And if you're fresh, I'll change your spines into chicken feathers."

"Come on now," said the hare soothingly. "We haven't done anything, have we? Can't you free us again with your witchcraft?"

"I can, but I'm not going to. Can't you take a joke?"

The hare and the hedgehog looked at each other. "What are we going to do now?" whispered the hedgehog.

The hare winked. He brushed some doughnut icing from his fur and said amicably, "Witch dear, I almost forgot. A very happy New Year!"

"The same to you," said the witch, a little surprised.

"Made any New Year's resolutions this year? Oh no, how silly I am. Witches don't do that, of course."

"Yes, they do," said the witch. "At least, I always do."

"Well, I don't," said the hedgehog. "I—"

The hare gave him a nudge. "How good you are," said the hare admiringly to the witch. "I would never have thought you did. And what were your resolutions?"

"Well, just the usual. Not to be so impatient, not to torment the animals . . ."

"Didn't I tell you! Nothing will come of that," said the hedgehog mockingly.

"Oh no?" cried the witch. "You'll soon find out. I think I'll change your spines into chicken feathers right now!"

"He means," said the hare quickly, "that it's a bit strange. You don't want to torment anymore, but in the meantime you throw a net over us and hold us prisoner."

"Yes! Isn't it a good joke?" The witch chuckled. "Oh, wait a minute, you mean—Is that tormenting? And that's just what I wasn't going to do . . ."

The witch thought about it. Then she sighed deeply.

"This is the last time. I'm not going to make good resolutions again. They spoil your pleasure. Ugh!" She mumbled a magic spell. Suddenly the net was loose. The witch gathered it up. "Bye," she said gloomily.

"Have a doughnut," said the hare.

"Thank you." The witch walked home munching. She dragged the net along behind her.

"Phew, all's well that ends well," said the hare, relieved.

"Well done," said the hedgehog. "We did that very cleverly together. How uncomfortable she looked."

The hare nodded. "Now do you see that good resolutions do make sense?"

"Yes," said the hedgehog. "I'm going to make a list myself right away. And do you know what? I'll have a doughnut after all!"

THE BOOK OF MAGIC

The owl flew high above the wood. Flying was still the safest, the higher the better, and even then you were not sure of being safe. The wood below seemed deserted. The owl sighed. No, the animals had not had an easy time recently. And that was because of the wicked witch, of course.

What a bad mood she had been in during the past few weeks. She had played one nasty trick after another. She had turned three squirrels into wood-mice, she had turned all the rabbits blue, she had strewn forget-powder and squirted vanishing water into the stream . . . The animals kept themselves hidden as much as possible. Everyone was frightened.

Look, there's the witch, there below, what's she doing now? Oh, she's looking for herbs. That's a bad sign. Hastily the owl spread his wings and flew away.

Later he was flying over the witch's cottage. A thick, smelly smoke rose out of the chimney. Inside, another nasty potion was probably simmering . . . But what was that? Something was moving there among the ferns, it looked like—Yes! It was the hare and the hedgehog who were creeping closer. Strange. The owl had

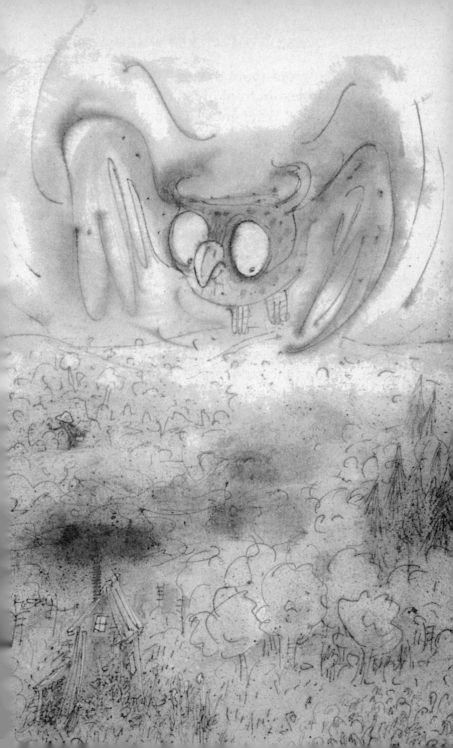

to find out more about that. He swooped down and landed just in front of his friends.

"Hey there! What are you doing?"

"Oh, brother!" squeaked the hedgehog, and he dropped flat on the ground.

The hare stumbled and scrambled angrily to his feet again. "Shh!" he hissed urgently. "Can't you keep your voice down?"

"I'm scared stiff," panted the hedgehog. "You and your big ideas!"

"I was just wondering what you were doing here," said the owl, taken aback.

"Shh!" whispered the hare. "The witch will hear us in a minute and then we'll have had it."

"She's way over there," said the owl, pointing. "Beyond the sandbank."

The hare breathed a sigh of relief. "Good. Then we still have time." He looked around quickly. "Owl, we're going to do something about it, the hedgehog and I."

"Do something about what?"

"About all the witch's tormenting. We're going to steal her book of magic!"

"B-b-book of magic," stammered the startled owl.

"Yes! Then she can't annoy us anymore. She knows only a few magic spells by heart, but all the recipes for those potions and powders are written in that book."

"And where will you put it?"

"At my place, in the cupboard."

"But—if she finds it . . ."

"She'll never find it there," said the hedge-hog. "She can't very well go looking in all the animals' cupboards!"

"Hurry up," said the hare. "She could be here any minute now. Owl, you keep watch. Hedgehog, we're going after it!"

Feeling uneasy, the owl flew onto the roof of the tumbledown cottage. Inside, there was the sound of stumbling and whispering. If only they would hurry up!

Oh, now there's going to be trouble. In the distance, the owl saw a pointed hat appear above the bushes . . .

He stamped on the roof. "She's coming! Let's go!"

The cottage door flew open. The hare and the hedgehog ran outside dragging a big, thick book. "Delay her!" they cried. Stumbling and panting, they disappeared into the wood.

Just in time! There came the witch shuffling nearer with a basket full of leafy plants on her arm. Without looking up, she shuffled into the cottage and slammed the door shut behind her.

The owl hid behind a large tree. He waited, his heart beating. When would she notice?

"Oohoo oohoo oohoo!" A piercing noise came suddenly from inside the cottage. "My book of magic! Thieves! Burglars! Oohoo oohoo

oohoo!"

The witch rushed outside. Stamping her feet, she stood in front of the door. She looked round furtively.

"You there! Owl!"

The owl felt his wings become clammy with fright. She had seen him.

"Owl, come here or I'll change you into a cockroach!"

Trembling, the owl flew to her.

"Where is it?" screamed the witch. "Tell me!"

"What?" whispered the owl almost soundlessly.

"My book of magic is gone! Do you perhaps know anything about it?"

"Abso . . . abso . . . no, really not, no," stammered the owl.

"Have you seen anyone near my cottage?"

"No no, or yes, wait a minute, actually yes."

"Who did you see?"

"Someone, a man, a gentleman or something. That direction, over there." He pointed to the back of the cottage.

"Did the gentleman have anything with him?"

"Er, yes, something under his arm, I think. Something brown."

"How big?"

"About as big as a big book."

"My book of magic!" screamed the witch.

She turned around and ran away in the direction the owl had pointed.

The owl fanned himself with his wings to cool down. What a fright! And he was such a bad liar. But anyway, she was out of the way for a while now. The owl turned and flew to the hare's house.

"The witch is furious!" called the owl breathlessly when he went inside. "But I sent her off in the opposite direction."

The hare and the hedgehog were not listening. They were sitting in front of the cupboard reading the book of magic.

"Owl, come and have a look," said the hedgehog. "All these recipes, and they're so complicated!"

"Not this one. VANISHING WATER," read the hare excitedly. "I've got all these things here, and the plants that have to go in grow just in front of the door."

"That's so simple. We could make it ourselves."

The hare and the hedgehog looked at each other. "Shall we? Just to try it . . ."

"Don't do it," said the owl. "It'll only cause trouble."

But the others had already started, and soon a pan was simmering on the fire. A strange smell spread through the room.

Shaking his head, the owl sat in a corner. The steam caught his throat. "Can I open a window?" he asked.

"No!" cried the hare, shocked. "If the witch smells it, we've had it!" He stirred a little more and then took the pan from the fire.

"Ready! Here's the vanishing water. If you throw this over somebody, he'll disappear. Presto! Gone."

An uneasy silence fell.

"Come on," said the hedgehog, pretending to be cheerful. "What shall we make disappear?"

"The book of magic," said the owl sourly.

"You must be nuts; that'd be a pity."

"This plate here," said the hare. He put the plate in the middle of the table and held the pan above it, hesitating.

"May I, hare? Let me do it," said the hedgehog, and he grabbed at the pan.

"Leave it alone," said the hare and stepped back.

"Hey, I made that stuff as well. Give it here!"

"Give that pan to me!" said the owl nervously. "An accident will happen any minute."

The hedgehog jumped at the pan, the hare held it high up in the air, the pan tipped over . . . and all the vanishing water poured over the hedgehog. The hedgehog felt himself becoming dizzy. He closed his eyes.

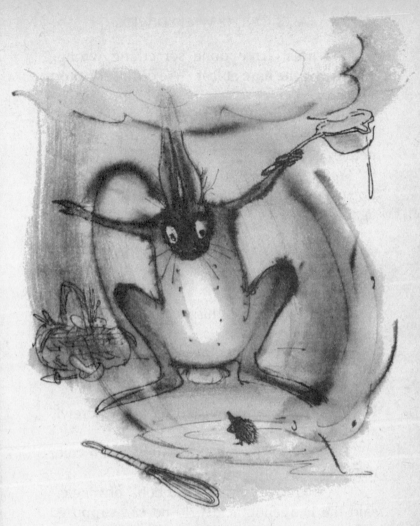

When he opened them again, the room had
become very big. He looked up. His friends
were very big too.

The hare and the owl, their eyes nearly pop-
ping out of their heads, looked at the very tiny
hedgehog on the middle of the mat.

"We must have done something wrong," whispered the hare at last. "We didn't stir properly or something."

"Terrible," muttered the owl. "Although it's not that bad. You could have disappeared altogether."

"You call this not too bad?" piped the hedgehog. "You must all see to it that I get bigger again!" and angry, he walked outside.

A few days later, the owl and the hedgehog sat gloomily in the sun, not far away from the hare's house.

"Being small like this is no picnic," complained the hedgehog.

"It gets more ridiculous every day," sighed the owl. "Look at that tree in front of the hare's house."

"The trunk is as twisted as a corkscrew!" cried the hedgehog.

"And all the rabbits are a light green color now," said the owl, shuddering.

"The hare's trying out the book of magic," said the hedgehog acidly. "And *he's* supposed to be our friend. Huh!"

"This can't go on any longer," said the owl. "That book has to go."

"And what about me then? And all the rabbits? There's still a slight chance the hare will change us back."

"Or he'll cause even more trouble. The witch is bound to notice that as well. The witch . . . ," continued the owl pensively. "*She* could change you back again."

"She could, yes, but if she finds out that I've stolen her book, it won't be the happiest day of my life."

"I've got it, I think," said the owl. "We'll steal the book from the hare and we'll give it back to the witch. On the condition that she puts right all that the hare has upset."

"She'll never do it," said the hedgehog gloomily. "I know *her*. And how would you steal the book? The hare never leaves his house anymore."

"I'll go and knock on the door. As soon as it opens, you slip inside and hide. You're so small, the hare will never notice. I'll try and get hold of the book, but if I don't manage it, you can open the door tonight when the hare is asleep, and then we'll get it."

The hedgehog got up. "We can only try."

A short while later, the owl knocked at the door of the hare's house. At first nothing happened. But when the owl knocked again, the door opened. A horrible smell billowed out.

"Ah, hare," said the owl, "how are you?" Meanwhile, the hedgehog slipped inside the house and crawled under the cupboard.

The hare blinked nervously. "Not so good,"

he said. "Terrible. But come inside quickly; otherwise the witch will smell something. Not that it'll make much difference, but . . ."

"What are you making?" asked the owl as he walked inside.

"Vanishing water."

The owl shrank back.

"You needn't be afraid. It's for me."

"For you?"

"Yes," said the hare with a sigh. "Everything has gone wrong. First the hedgehog became small because of me. And after that I kept trying to make him big again. I thought I'd got the right magic spell, but then all the rabbits turned green. And when I tried something else, the tree trunk became twisted. I can't do it. And now I'm putting an end to it. Vanishing water over myself and—gone."

"But . . . but . . . ," said the owl, shocked.

He could not say any more because suddenly the door was thrown open. The wicked witch stood in the doorway.

"Aha!" she screamed. "I can smell it. Vanishing water. Incompetent that you are. Bungler! Give me my book of magic!"

The hare was unable to utter a word. But the owl quickly stepped in front of the pan with the vanishing water and said as firmly as possible, "You'll get your book. But then you'll have to change back all that has accidentally gone wrong."

"Definitely not. Give that book here or I'll change you both into yellow-edged water beetles."

The owl took the pan off the fire. "If you don't put right all that the hare has ruined, then I'll throw this water all over your book of magic!"

"Don't do that," cried the witch. She took her magic wand out of her apron, waved it around, and mumbled something.

The hedgehog under the cupboard felt himself getting very dizzy. And then he bumped his head badly.

"Ow!" he cried, and he crept rather dazedly from under the cupboard.

"Hedgehog!" said the surprised hare. "Where did you come from all of a sudden? And . . . and you're big again!"

The owl looked outside. "The tree is straight again as well. And look, there goes a brown rabbit."

"The vanishing water has also disappeared," said the witch. "Now I want my book of magic back. And make it quick!"

"Here you are!" cried the hare and the owl and the hedgehog, all at the same time. "Take it with you. And thank you again. How clever you are. Thank you!"

The witch blushed. She took the book and ran home with it.

The three friends looked at one another, their eyes beaming.

"I'm big again," said the hedgehog.

"Everything is back as it was before," said the owl.

"I've got rid of that wretched book," said the hare.

THE WICKED WITCH IS ILL

It was raining. The hare and the hedgehog were sheltering under a bush.

"It keeps on raining," said the hedgehog, down in the dumps.

"All the same, we're dry here," said the hare. "I think it's pleasant, raindrops dripping on the leaves."

"Oh, oh!" shrieked the hedgehog.

"What's the matter? What's the matter?"

"A raindrop dripped on my neck!" said the hedgehog angrily. "Pleasant, yes, but getting soaked is something else."

"You're in a really bad mood. Are you worried about something?"

"No, but we're very near the wicked witch's cottage. That's why I want the rain to stop—then we could leave."

"The wicked witch," said the hare thoughtfully. "I was just thinking about her this morning. I haven't seen her for a long time."

"You should be pleased," said the hedgehog. "The less you see of her, the better it is for your health."

"When did you last see her?"

"Let me think. Last week, I believe. No, now that you mention it, I haven't seen her for a long time either."

"Could she be ill?"

The hedgehog shrugged his shoulders. "Then she can make herself better again. Plenty of magic spells."

"Maybe she's fallen and has broken something."

"And maybe she's cooking up a very mean trick to make all our lives difficult."

The hare shuffled restlessly to and fro. "All the same, I'll go and have a peek. After all, it's very near here. It's possible something awful has happened. Sometimes, you know, she's quite nice."

"Pity that doesn't happen more often," mumbled the hedgehog.

"Are you coming with me?"

"*Me?* What do you take me for? That woman put knots in my spines once; I don't trust her at all. No, you go on your own."

The dripping on the leaves stopped. The hare looked out. "Dry," he declared. "Well, I'm off." He waited a minute. "I must go," he said. He took a deep breath. "I'm going!" and he jumped out.

Shaking his head, the hedgehog watched him go. "Idiot. He is far too trusting. He'll go into her house, of course, just like that, and then I bet we'll never see him again . . . HARE!" he called out with all his might.

The hare stood still.

"Wait a minute. I'll go with you after all. But I still think it's madness."

"Good," said the hare, pleased. "Come on, let's go."

A short while later, they stood in front of the witch's cottage. The hare knocked on the door. There was no answer.

The hare knocked again.

"Who's there?" called a weak voice.

"The hare and the hedgehog."

"Come in. I'm ill."

"There, I told you so, didn't I?" whispered the hare.

"It could be a trap," the hedgehog hissed back. "As soon as we're inside, she'll take us prisoner."

The hare shrugged his shoulders and stepped inside. Reluctantly the hedgehog followed.

It was stuffy in the cottage. The witch lay on the bed under a thick blanket. She looked very pale.

"What do you want?" she asked hoarsely.

"We hadn't seen you for a long time," said the hare, "and we were worried. Can we help?"

"Don't you have a magic spell to make yourself better?" asked the hedgehog.

"Yes," said the witch, "but there's an herbal potion to go with it. It's almost ready, but elder flowers and beech leaves have to go in. I haven't got those and I'm too ill to go out."

"We'll get them," said the hare. "And if you tell me how to do it later, I'll finish making the potion as well. Are you coming, hedgehog?"

"It's raining again . . . ," said the hedgehog.

"All right. Then you stay here. I'll be back soon."

The hedgehog looked nervously at the witch and said, "No no, a little rain won't do any harm. I'll go with you."

It was not long before they were back. The hare had the elder flowers and the beech leaves with him, and the hedgehog carried a big bouquet of flowers.

"Here we are again," cried the hare, and he shook the rain off his fur. "Tell me how to make that potion, then the hedgehog will take care of the food."

The witch gave instructions in a hoarse voice. Very soon there were good smells in the little room—it smelled of herbs and food. When the potion was ready, the witch took a few large gulps and mumbled a magic spell.

The hedgehog pricked up his ears, but he could not understand any of it.

"Hey," said the witch. "I feel much better already. In a few days I'll have recovered completely."

"Take it easy at first," warned the hare. "You'll still be weak."

"That's true. It will take weeks before I can turn someone into a pine cone again."

"You shouldn't start doing that too soon," said the hedgehog quickly. "It can be very dangerous. And move that magic stuff away. The food is ready."

It was still raining when the hare and the hedgehog walked home.

"Shall we go and help again tomorrow?" asked the hare. "She can't do much herself for the time being."

The hedgehog nodded and said, "For the time being, she can't do any more witchcraft, thank goodness!"

THE HARE WANTS TO BE ALONE

The hare stood in front of his house and wiped his brow. What a day! First the crow had dropped by with a story that had taken hours to tell, then the owl had come with plans for a party, after that a whole mole family had landed on his doorstep to ask if he knew of a house for them, and they still had not left when the blackbird came in. And so it went. And not only today. Day in, day out, it was the same story.

"All this bustle is driving me mad," grumbled the hare. "Let's see, the only person I haven't seen today is the wicked witch."

"Yoo-hoo," screeched a sharp voice. "You're looking very fed up!"

"That's all I need," said the hare. "I mean, hello, witch, good afternoon, witch, I'm rather tired, that's all."

"Then you should have a rest. Shall I change you into a pine cone? That's very peaceful, hi hi, ha ha."

Chuckling, the witch went on her way.

"Nasty woman," mumbled the hare. "But she's right. I need a rest. Alone. No fuss around me for a little while."

He stared ahead, thinking. Suddenly he turned around and ran inside his house. When the hare came out a little later, he had a small suitcase with him. He stuck a note on the door:

NOT AT HOME — FOR A LONG TIME

and he looked around. There was no one to be seen. He began to tiptoe down the wood-path. If he went very quietly, no one would notice that he was leaving. Otherwise, everyone would know where he was and that would—

"Hey!" said a voice just above his head. The hare jumped in the air and, pale with fright, looked up. The blackbird sat on a twig, watching him suspiciously.

"You're acting very sly. Have you maybe stolen something?"

"Shh, shh, shh!" said the hare. "Don't talk so loud!"

"What's going on?" said the blackbird. "You were acting strange this morning, come to think of it, but this is going too far. What's in that suitcase?"

"Sandwiches," said the hare. "And my drawing things. I'm going away."

"Away? Why? Where to?"

"I need a rest!" snapped the hare. "I want to be alone."

"Goodness me," said the blackbird. "You won't last more than a day. Wouldn't it be better to go to bed early?"

"No. I don't want to see anyone for the time being. Not for at least a few weeks."

"I bet you'll be back home tomorrow."

"Oh no! You won't see me back for some time. Goodbye!"

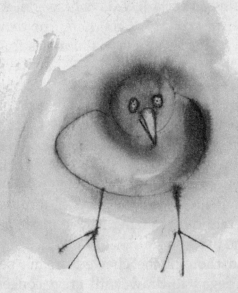

Annoyed, the hare went off down the path.

Shaking his head, the blackbird watched him go. "This won't come to anything," he said softly. "He won't last. I'll have to keep an eye on things." He flew behind the hare at a safe distance to see where he was going.

The hare had not noticed anything. He walked on at a steady pace for quite a long time until he came to a spot that seemed to him to be lonely enough. He sat down, opened his suitcase, and began to eat a sandwich. "Peace and quiet," said the hare, satisfied.

The hare was very happy on his own. He went on long walks and made piles of drawings.

Nevertheless, after a few days he began to feel restless. How are the others doing? he thought. Are they missing me? Have the moles found a house? Oh, why should I care? I'm having a lovely vacation.

He took his sketchbook and his pencils and began to draw a tree. But his thoughts were elsewhere. And after a while he noticed that he had not drawn a tree at all but rather a bird, and that the bird looked exactly like the blackbird.

"Look at me," said the hare. "I am absent-minded. Without realizing it, I've made a portrait of the blackbird!"

Lost in thought, he chewed on his pencil. Then he began to draw with great concentration. Next to the blackbird came the owl, and next to him the hedgehog with the bat and the squirrel and the crow. The entire sheet of paper became crammed full of all the animals he knew. And right at the top, in the corner, he drew the wicked witch on a broomstick. Then he laid his sketchbook on the floor, and slowly he started on a walk.

The hare had not gone far when the blackbird came flying along. Curious, he looked at the drawing. "I thought as much!" he sniffed. "He's homesick. All his friends are in it. Even the wicked witch, and he has given her a friendly face too. He must be in a very bad way. Poor thing."

The blackbird was startled when he heard slow footsteps behind him. As quick as he could, he fluttered away and called over his shoulder, "Hey hare, I came along by chance. I'm going now because you will want to be alone. See you in a few weeks." And off he went.

The hare watched him go and blinked his eyes. "A few weeks. How am I going to last that long!"

He looked at his drawing. "I miss you," he said sadly. He sat down. "Of course I can just go back, but then the blackbird would say 'I told you so'!"

He sighed and gazed ahead. Slowly it began to get dark. The hare was still sitting in the same place. Suddenly he saw a light in the distance. The light was moving. And behind that came another light and another one. There were lots and lots. They came nearer and nearer, and the hare could hear singing every now and then. It looked like a procession.

He stood up so that he could see better. The lights were still approaching, and now the hare could distinguish the first faces. That looked like . . . that was the blackbird walking in front. And behind him, with lanterns, came the hedgehog, the owl, the squirrel, and all the animals he knew!

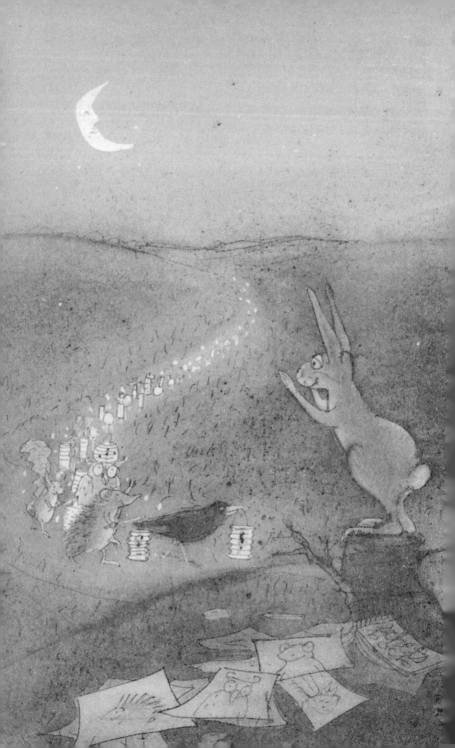

"Hello!" cried the hare as loud as he could. "Hello, everybody!"

The procession was now close by; the singing was deafening.

"Stop!" shouted the blackbird. Everyone stopped. "Hare," said the blackbird. "You'll probably be upset that we've come to disturb you when you are alone—"

"Not at all!" cried the hare.

"—but there's a big party this evening. The mole family has finally found a house and we're going to celebrate it. We wanted to ask if you will come because you gave them good advice."

"I'd very much like to come to your party," said the hare, beaming.

The blackbird winked. "If you like, you can come straight back to be alone again tomorrow. Then—"

"Definitely not," said the hare quickly. "I'm going home with you and I'm staying home."

"Are you quite sure you don't need any more rest, hmm?"

The hare and the blackbird looked at each other. Then they both began to laugh.

"Come on," said the blackbird, and he patted the hare on his shoulder. "Otherwise the party will be starting late."

"I'll just get my things," said the hare. "And—and . . . I've missed you terribly."

"Hooray!" cheered the animals. They turned around and the procession started again. Back toward home. On the way the hare chatted with everyone. He even greeted the wicked witch when they passed her cottage. And at the party he danced so much that his muscles ached for days.

A BAD MOOD IN THE MORNING

The hare got up very early one morning. He jumped out of his house, looked around, and said, "Ah! I bet it's going to be a beautiful day."

He hopped a few times, got a head start, and jumped over a tree stump.

"Yippee!" cried the hare. "A good run!"

He ran as fast as he could along the stream. But who was that standing there pondering on the bank? It was the hedgehog.

"Hey, hedgehog! You're up early too! What are you doing?"

"Nothing," said the hedgehog gloomily.

"Nothing, why's that? I'm having a good run and I was just thinking, what a pity that no one's running with me. Do you feel like coming for a run?"

"No."

Rather agitated now, the hare circled round the hedgehog. "What's the matter?"

"Nothing."

"Did you sleep badly? Did you have a bad dream? Are you ill?"

"No!" cried the hedgehog. "And leave me alone! You're irritating me with all that jumping about!"

"But what's the matter then?"

"I'm in a bad mood," said the hedgehog. "And if you want to know, I'm like this every morning. Go away now, please."

"In a bad mood in the morning? You mean you're grumpy until about eleven o'clock? Or until what time are you like that?"

"About eleven o'clock."

The hare shook his head. "I've never noticed it. But now that I think about it, I always see you late in the morning. Or in the afternoon."

"Now you know why," said the hedgehog curtly.

The hare did not know quite what to do, so he was pleased to see the blackbird calmly flying toward them.

"Good morning," said the blackbird as he landed. "How are you both?"

"Fine," said the hare.

"Hmm," said the hedgehog.

Surprised, the blackbird looked at him. "What's the matter with you?"

"He's in one of his early morning bad moods," explained the hare.

"That's a shame," said the blackbird. "Are you like that every morning?"

"Yoo-hoo!" cried a sharp voice just behind them. "Yoo-hoo!"

"The wicked witch!" said the hare and the blackbird, frightened. Quickly they moved aside.

The hedgehog remained standing stock-still.

"When you've just about had enough, *she* shows up," he grumbled.

The witch looked at him with disapproval. "Did you get out of bed on the wrong side?"

"An early morning bad mood," said the hare and the blackbird.

"So what?" said the witch. "I'm always in a mood like that, all day. Yoo-hoo, hedgehog, give me a smile, hi hi, ha ha!"

"Make yourself scarce, you!" cried the hedgehog, stiffening all his spines.

"Now now, what's all this? Calm down or I'll turn you into a pine cone." But the witch sounded a bit uncertain.

The hedgehog gazed at her intently. The gaze was so nasty that the witch shrunk back with fright.

"Come on, witch, come on, blackbird," said the hare. "We should leave the hedgehog in peace. Come with me to my house. I don't feel like running anymore now."

Some time later, the three of them were sitting in front of the hare's house. The hare had prepared a meal, but nobody had much appetite. The witch was just staring straight ahead, bewildered.

They were still sitting in the sun when they heard someone singing in the distance. The singing became louder and louder. It went like this: "As long as a hedgehog has his spines, he has nothing at all to fear."

"That'll be him," whispered the witch. And yes, there came the hedgehog strolling along, singing loudly.

"Hello!" he cried. "I thought you'd still be sitting here. Is there any food left?"

"More than enough," said the hare. "How are you feeling now?"

"Fine, thank you. What a lovely day today.

Life is marvelous after eleven o'clock in the morning."

"Before eleven o'clock too," said the blackbird. "Although some people don't see it like that."

The hedgehog kicked a stone shyly. "I can't help it," he said. "Was I very unpleasant?"

"I'll say!" said the witch.

The hedgehog kicked another stone. "That's just the way I am in the morning. But I'll make up for it. Will you come and have a bite to eat at my place tomorrow?"

"Gladly," said the hare.

"With pleasure," said the blackbird.

"Very nice," said the witch.

They looked at one another.

"But after eleven o'clock!" all three said at the same time.

THE HEDGEHOG HEARS GHOSTS

Deep in the wood, a short distance past the wicked witch's cottage, there is a small pool. For some time now, the wildest stories have been going around about this pool.

"It's haunted," whispered the hedgehog, who was sitting under a bush with the hare and the blackbird.

"What did you say?" asked the hare, shocked.

"Nonsense," mumbled the blackbird. "He's at it again. Now it's haunted all of a sudden."

"Not all of a sudden," said the hedgehog angrily. "I used to like going there but during the last few weeks . . . ooh!"

"But what exactly happens near the pool?" asked the hare.

"Voices," said the hedgehog. "You keep hearing voices, and then if you look, there's no one there. And strange bubbling noises, like *blub blub blub*. And stares. I mean, you don't see anyone but you can feel them watching you."

"Nonsense," muttered the blackbird. "Imagination."

"Strange," said the hare. "We'll have to investigate."

"If you'll come with me, I don't mind," said the hedgehog. "But you won't get me going there again on my own."

"I pass," said the blackbird. "I'm not going to look at your will-o'-the-wisps. It doesn't bother me."

"Oh . . . ," said the hedgehog slowly. "You're not coming. And shall I tell you why not? You're frightened, you scaredy-cat!"

"Scaredy-cat! You'll soon find out, I . . ."

"Come on now," said the hare quickly. "You know what we'll do? We'll all go to the pool now, the three of us. I'll go first."

The blackbird and the hedgehog gave each other nasty looks and then walked behind the hare.

Nobody spoke on the way, not until they came to the pool.

"We're here," said the hare.

"Those ghosts of yours," said the blackbird. "So where are they?"

"Shh, shh!" hissed the hedgehog. "Can't you feel the strange atmosphere here?"

"I can't feel anything, I can only feel my feet because I've walked so far. Do you have any more great ideas like this!"

Blub blub blub, came a bubbling sound from the pool.

"There!" cried the hedgehog. "Didn't I tell you?"

"It's probably a frog," said the blackbird. But he sounded a little hesitant.

"It's as if we're being watched," said the hare in a low voice. "But I can't see anyone."

"We're in danger standing here," whispered the blackbird. "Let's go and hide behind that tree."

They tiptoed to the tree and waited. *Blub blub blub*, they heard again. And then splashing noises.

"Listen," whispered the hedgehog.

Above the splashing noises, you could hear

soft voices.

"I think this is really scary," said the hare.

"Now do you believe it's haunted, black-bird?"

The blackbird shrugged his shoulders.

"Well done, keep it up, go on!" cried a deep voice suddenly.

"Oh, brother!" piped the hedgehog. The hare tried not to listen.

The blackbird peeped carefully from behind the tree trunk and said softly, "Well, I never."

For there on the banks of the pool stood a big frog, and in the pool was the wicked witch, swimming with awkward movements.

"Well done!" cried the frog.

The blackbird gave the hare and the hedge-hog a push and said, "Come and have a look, here are your ghosts!" He came out from behind the tree and fluttered to the water. "What's this, are you having a swimming les-son?"

The witch gave a squawk of fright and sank underwater straightaway—*blub blub blub*—then came up again and crossly spit out a mouthful of water.

"Thanks a lot!" she cried sharply. "I was just getting the hang of it and then you come along and scare me to death. I'll wrap you in a spi-der's web, I'll—"

"You're swimming very well," said the

blackbird quickly.

"Do you think so?" asked the witch, flattered.

"I certainly do," said the blackbird. "Splendid!" He held his wing in front of his beak and tried not to laugh.

Reluctantly, the hare and the hedgehog came closer and said, "Splendid, yes, very good."

The witch turned pink with pride. With difficulty she dragged herself out of the water.

"So that's what the noises were," said the hedgehog. "You've been taking swimming lessons from the frog here."

"Yes," said the witch, "for a few weeks now. But I didn't want anyone to know about it."

"Why not?" asked the blackbird.

"Because you would all come and make fun of me."

"We never make fun of anyone!" cried the hare.

The witch looked at him suspiciously. "I just want to learn how to swim without anyone interfering. So if anyone comes, I dive away behind those tall reeds there."

"Blub blub blub," mumbled the blackbird.

"We thought it was haunted here," said the hedgehog.

"*You* thought that," said the blackbird indignantly. "*I* didn't!"

The witch spluttered it out. "Haunted!" she

scoffed. "What an idea. Ghosts that swim, I suppose!"

The hedgehog looked down.

"Well," said the witch, "I'm going to put on some dry things. See you tomorrow, frog." And still chuckling, she shuffled back to her cottage.

The frog croaked goodbye and jumped into the water.

The blackbird slapped the hedgehog on his shoulder. "Didn't I tell you? It isn't scary here at all. You shouldn't let yourself get frightened so easily, you!"

The hedgehog wanted to say something back, but the hare said quickly, "Are you coming home with me? It's getting late."

The hare and the blackbird walked in front; the hedgehog trudged behind.

Suddenly the hedgehog started walking on tiptoe. He crept forward until he was just behind the blackbird. Then he said in a hollow voice, "Blub blub blub!"

"Help!" piped the blackbird, and he jumped aside with a flutter.

The hedgehog slapped him on the shoulder.

"You shouldn't let yourself get frightened so easily, you," he said.

WITCH'S DAY

Deep in thought, the hare walked along the trail. He was thinking about his birthday. It was not his birthday for a few months yet, but he was already thinking about the gifts that he would like to receive and who he was going to invite and that sort of thing. He was so deep in thought that he did not hear shuffling footsteps coming nearer.

"Hey there, hare!" cried a sharp voice.

The hare cringed. Carefully he looked around. Behind him stood the wicked witch. She had a big bunch of withered branches under her arm.

"Help me carry these, please," she said.

"I didn't hear you coming," said the hare.

"No, otherwise you'd have run away," chuckled the witch. "But now that you're here anyway, you can help."

Together they carried the heavy branches to the witch's cottage.

"Put them in the corner," said the witch. "And throw a few branches on the fire."

She looked into a large pan that hung simmering over the fire. The hare sniffed approvingly. "Smells good. What are you making?"

"Currant juice," said the witch. She took a ladle and started stirring.

The hare stared at the flames. Suddenly he asked, "When exactly is your birthday?"

"Birthday?" said the witch. "Witches never have birthdays."

"That can't be true," said the hare. "After all, you were born, weren't you? Then after that, you have a birthday every year."

The witch stirred the pan and mumbled something.

"What did you say?" asked the hare.

"I said that I don't know when it's my birthday because witches never celebrate their birthdays. They don't do that."

"Why not?"

"They just don't."

"Don't you think that's a pity?" asked the

hare. "No presents, no decorations, no happy-birthday-to-you, no party?"

"Get out of here," shrieked the witch. "You're keeping me from my work with all your drivel. Go!" And she lashed out at the hare with her ladle.

"I'm going," cried the hare. He jumped outside and ran home.

When the hare arrived at his house, the owl and the hedgehog were waiting for him in front of the door. "Where have you come from?" they asked.

"From the witch," panted the hare. "Listen . . ." And he told them what had happened to him. "So she never celebrates her birthday," he concluded.

"Does that surprise you?" asked the hedgehog. "Who would there be to visit her on her birthday? *We* wouldn't go for anything, and her sister in the south lives much too far away."

"No birthday visitors," said the hare dejectedly. "No presents, no happy-birthday-to-you. It's so sad."

"She has only herself to blame," said the owl.

"Yes, but still," said the hare.

"She should have been nicer," said the hedgehog. "It's her own fault."

"Yes, but still."

"So what do you want to do about it?" asked

the owl. "Give her a present?"

"Something like that, yes. And sing. And decorate her cottage with streamers."

"And all of us get bewitched, I suppose," sniffed the hedgehog. "You go and get on with your streamers. I'm not going with you."

"But when?" asked the owl. "If she doesn't know when it's her birthday herself."

"We'll just choose a day," said the hare. "And that will be Witch's Day."

"Witch's Day?"

"Yes. You have Pets' Day, don't you? Why not Witch's Day?"

"When is it Hedgehog Day?" asked the hedgehog.

The hare looked at him accusingly.

"I mean, when is it Witch's Day?" asked the hedgehog quickly.

"Tomorrow, right away!" said the hare.

The next morning the witch was very busy. She had poured currant juice into bottles and now she was crushing herb powder in a large mortar. If she put some of that powder in the currant juice and then let the animals drink it, then the fun would begin. She chuckled at the thought.

Suddenly she stopped crushing. She heard rustling outside. No, it was quiet again. But what was that? There was loud singing outside:

"For she's a jolly good fellow, for she's a jolly good fellow, and so say all of us!"

The witch left the mortar and opened the door. There stood the hare, the owl, and the hedgehog singing at the top of their voices. "Hip, hip, hooray!" they cried. "Hip, pip, pip! Congratulations! All the very best!"

"For what?" asked the witch suspiciously.

"For Witch's Day!" said the hare.

"Witch's Day!" said the witch. "That doesn't exist. Never heard of it."

"It's today, for the first time," explained the hare. "Because witches don't celebrate birthdays. Look, we've decorated your cottage."

The witch looked round. Streamers were hanging in the ivy. She nodded grimly. "So that was the rustling. Take all that mess away. And get lost! Witch's Day. Huh!"

"Wait a minute now," said the hare. "The owl has made a poem. Let's hear it, owl."

The owl cleared his throat. He looked shyly at the wicked witch and began in an unsteady voice:

"Today is Witch's Day.
That's why we're all so gay.
That the witch's life a long one will be
Is a wish expressed by all of we."

The witch turned very red and looked for her handkerchief.

"That last bit should really be 'of us,'" ex-

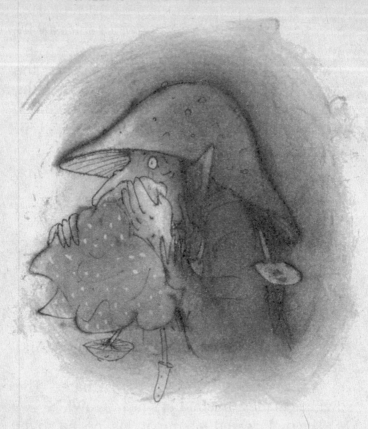

plained the owl nervously. "But that doesn't rhyme, you see."

"It's so beautiful like that," said the witch hoarsely. "Nobody has ever made a poem for me before."

"Has anyone ever baked a fruit cake for you before?" asked the hedgehog. "Here, and happy Witch's Day." He pushed a plate into the witch's hands and stepped back quickly.

"Fruit cake," said the witch. "How delicious. Would you like fruit cake with currant juice? Come inside."

The hedgehog and the owl looked at each other.

"Well no, actually . . . ," said the hedgehog.

"I should really, uh . . . ," said the owl.

"We'd love to, just for a minute," said the hare quickly, and he stepped inside.

Reluctantly the other two followed.

"Sit down," said the witch. She poured out the currant juice and began to cut the fruit cake. The hedgehog strolled round the cottage and looked curiously into the big mortar.

"What's in there?" he asked.

"That has to go into the currant juice," said the witch absent-mindedly.

The hedgehog took some herb powder out of the mortar and sprinkled it into his glass. He took a sip and made a face. "Ugh, bitter," he said. He sat down quickly.

Shocked, the witch looked up. "Oohoo, oohoo!" she cried. "Have you touched that herb powder?"

The hedgehog nodded, pale with fright. He felt himself getting very light. He covered his eyes with his hands. When he dared to look again, he was floating high above his chair. "Oh, oh, oh . . . ," he said, frightened.

The hare and the owl looked up, horrified.

"Those magic spells all the time!" moaned the owl.

"This—this—I didn't mean for this to happen," stuttered the witch. "This morning I did, but not anymore, really not. He did it himself."

The hedgehog began flapping his paws and then he went floating through the room.

"Oh, oh!" he cried.

"Do something!" cried the hare to the wicked witch.

She shrugged her shoulders. "That's not necessary. It'll go away on its own. And I don't think he minds it so much."

"Whoopee!" cried the hedgehog. "Hare, hare, I can fly! Owl, look, I can fly just like you!"

"That's not flying," said the owl sourly. "You haven't even got wings." And shaking his head, he went and sat in the corner. The hare walked nervously around and talked excitedly about the weather and how to make a fruit cake. The witch only half listened to him. Softly mumbling, she learned "Today is Witch's Day" by heart. And the hedgehog floated and dived through the room, pulled on the hare's ears, pushed over the lamp, and crowed more mischievously all the time, "Whoopee!" But suddenly his feet began to tingle. "My feet are numb," he said.

The witch got a chair and put it right under

the hedgehog. The hedgehog felt himself getting very heavy, and he dropped into the chair.

"Whoopee," he said softly.

The hare and the owl heaved a sigh of relief
and quickly took another piece of fruit cake.

"I told you it would go away on its own,"
said the witch.

The hedgehog sighed deeply.

"Idiot," hissed the hare.

"Dimwit," mumbled the owl.

The hedgehog nodded dreamily. "I can fly,"
he said.

"Who would like some more currant juice?"
asked the witch.

The hedgehog jumped up. "Me!!"

"But without herb powder!" cried the hare
and the owl with their mouths full.

An hour later, full of currant juice and fruit
cake, the animals said goodbye. The witch
remained at the door for a while and watched
them go.

The blackbird flew by. Surprised by the
witch's expression, he said, "How happy you
seem. Has anything happened?"

The witch nodded and said, "Today is
Witch's Day!"

THE HARE'S BIRTHDAY

*When the hare woke up, he knew there was some-*thing special about today. But what? He lay thinking; then he remembered.

It was his birthday.

He stretched and jumped out of bed. "I must get a move on!" said the hare. "It might get busy around here."

He pushed the door wide open. They can come now, he thought.

Outside, it was very quiet.

The hare pushed the chairs against the wall, put a cake on the table and hung a streamer up.

Where were they? Usually they were very early.

He walked outside and stood waiting in front of the door.

He waited for a long time. Again and again he looked along the wood-path, but nobody came.

The hare went back inside. He took a piece of cake, but he did not enjoy it. He looked outside again. There was no one to be seen.

The hare shook his head. "They've all for-gotten," he said softly. He waited a while. Then he closed the door slowly.

He went and sat in a corner and stared

ahead sadly.

But what was that? He heard something outside. Full of hope, he looked toward the door.
There was a knock! The hare jumped up and
opened the door.

"At last!" he cried. "Where—" Shocked, he
stopped.

The wicked witch stood on the doorstep.

"Here," said the witch, and she pushed a
package into his hands. "You thought up
Witch's Day, so that's why you're getting something from me now."

"How nice!" said the hare. "Come inside,
would you like some cake? There's nobody else
here yet . . ."

The witch chuckled. "The others are coming
soon," she said. "I held them up for a bit
because I wanted to be the first and my present
wasn't ready."

"Held them up?" asked the hare. "How do
you mean?"

But before the witch could answer, loud
singing burst loose outside:

"Long live the hare
  Hip, hip, hooray!
  Three cheers for the hare,
  It's his birthday today."

The hare threw the door wide open. There

stood the owl, the hedgehog, the blackbird and the bat, the crow, the squirrel, three rabbits, the mole family . . .

"Hooray!" they cried. "May you have many more years to come!"

"What a beautiful song," said the hare, beaming. "That must be one of the owl's poems. Come inside, everyone!"

"We're a little late," said the owl. "But that's the wicked witch's fault. We were practicing our song—"

"—and then she enchanted us with her magic spell so that we couldn't move!" cried the hedgehog. "We couldn't move away from where we were. I'll get her for this! If I see her, then—" He stopped, turned pale, and looked at the witch.

"What will you do if you see me?" asked the witch.

"Then—then I'll run away fast," whispered the hedgehog. He turned around.

"Don't run away!" cried the hare. "I'm so happy that you're here. And the witch won't do anything—really she won't."

"I'm only eating cake," said the witch with her mouth full.

Hesitantly the animals came nearer.

"I've had a present from the witch," said the hare. "Look."

He opened the parcel.

"A scarf!" he cried. "How beautiful."

"I knitted it myself," said the witch. "You may well be needing it, hi hi, ha ha."

"Thank you," said the hare. "How does it look?" He threw the scarf round his neck and looked around proudly.

He saw the animals looking at him, amazed. "Is something the matter?" he asked.

Frightened, the animals looked at the place where the hare had just been standing. Because the hare was gone, completely disappeared, only the scarf hung in the air.

"Where are you?" piped the hedgehog.

"Here!" said the hare, surprised.

The witch began to splutter; she slapped her knees with laughter. "Look at those faces! Hi hi, ha ha!"

The owl went over to her threateningly. "That's enough of all that witchcraft! See to it that the hare comes back! And quickly!"

"He hasn't gone at all," chuckled the witch. "If he takes that scarf off, you'll be able to see him again."

The hedgehog ran forward and pulled at the scarf.

"What are you doing?" said the hare.

The animals sighed with relief. There stood the hare again, just like before.

"You were invisible!" they cried.

"Invisible? Me? Is that why you were looking at me so strangely?"

"I knitted a magic spell into it," explained the witch. "As a sort of surprise."

"How exciting," said the hare. "I'll try it again. But where is my scarf?"

"There! There it is, floating near the door," said the owl, pointing, and he dived forward. "Got it!"

"Ow!" cried the hedgehog, who had suddenly appeared near the door.

"You were taking my scarf!" said the hare indignantly.

"Only just to tr-try it," stammered the hedgehog.

"Yes, yes," said the owl severely. "Run off invisibly. Hmph!"

Ashamed, the hedgehog shuffled back.

"May I try too, hare, let me!" the others cried all at the same time. "Just for a minute, just to see what it's like."

"Oh, all right," said the hare. "Owl, you can try first."

"I don't want to," said the owl. He took a piece of cake and went and sat down as far away as possible from the wicked witch.

The other animals swarmed round the hare. In turn they tried on the scarf, and in turn they became invisible. Then cups floated through the air, pieces of cake disappeared, there was some pinching . . .

And the witch sat chuckling quietly and ate a whole cake all by herself.

The blackbird came and sat next to her. "What a good present," he said. "And so handy if you don't want to talk to anyone, or if you want to surprise someone . . ."

"Or if you want to steal something," said the owl sourly. He looked straight at the witch. "A magic potion or something."

The witch went pale. She mumbled to herself and got up.

"What did you say?" asked the hare.

"Nothing," said the witch. "I must go now," and she walked to the door.

The hare hung his scarf over a chair and went to open the door.

The owl got up as well. When no one was watching, he took the scarf, put it on, and tiptoed behind the witch.

"Where are you going, owl?" asked the hare. "I thought you didn't want to try my scarf?"

Shocked, the owl turned around. All the animals stared at him. He looked at himself. He was visible! Just as if he did not have the scarf on.

"Well, I'm blowed," yelped the hedgehog. "First you scold me, and then you want to go off with it yourself!"

"I . . . er . . . I," stammered the owl unhappily, "I wanted to give it back to the witch. That invisible business, it'll cause nothing but trouble."

"What trouble?" cried the hedgehog. "On the contrary, it's fun. You're always gloomy, you are."

The owl rubbed his chin thoughtfully. "Perhaps you're right," he said. "But wait a minute. The scarf doesn't work anymore. Look."

The witch nodded. "That was a spell that lasts for only a short time. A surprise for the party."

"Won't the spell work ever again?" asked the hedgehog, disappointed.

"No," said the witch curtly. "Because that causes trouble."

"Oh, darn," said the hedgehog. "That scarf's no use."

Annoyed, the witch looked at him. "It's lovely and warm," she snarled.

"And it's very beautiful," said the hare quickly.

The witch gave the hedgehog another angry glance and was about to walk outside. But the hedgehog pulled her skirt and asked coaxingly, "Witch, will you knit me a scarf with a magic spell in it as well?"

"And for me and for me too!" cried all the

others as they pushed their way toward the witch.

"I'm no fool," screeched the witch. "I've other things to do. Move aside, out of the way, all of you, or I'll make your ears invisible."

Shocked, the animals made room. The witch walked outside, and mumbling, she disappeared into the wood.

"She doesn't mean any harm," said the hare.

"You never know with her," said the blackbird with a sigh.

"Here's your scarf back," said the owl. "I'm so glad that no one will become invisible anymore."

The hare put his scarf on and walked to the mirror.

"Me too," he said, "because at last I can see now how it looks on me."

THE TRIP ROPE

Slowly, the owl walked through the wood. He looked very serious and he mumbled softly to himself: "Leaves are falling left and right, autumn is such a great delight."

The owl was making a poem.

"Snow lies on the trees so light, when winter comes and it's cold at night . . . The moon shines through the trees so bright . . ."

BOOM!

Suddenly he was lying flat in a big pile of leaves. He had tripped over something. He looked carefully. A rope had been stretched across the path just in front of the pile of leaves.

"What a mean trick," said the owl. "Who would do a thing like that?"

From behind the bushes he heard rustling and sniggering. He clambered up. "Who's there?" he cried angrily.

The blackbird and the hedgehog came from behind the bushes.

"Hey, owl," said the hedgehog. "Have you hurt yourself? No, eh?"

"No," said the owl. "But I did have a fright. And I was busy making a poem, a very beautiful poem, and now I've forgotten how it went."

"That'll come back to you again," said the blackbird, "that—"

"Someone else is coming," whispered the hedgehog. "Let's get out of here!"

They hid behind the bushes again.

The hare came strolling along the path. He was chewing on a blade of grass and was humming a song.

"Watch out, hare!" cried the owl. "There's a rope!"

The hare looked up absent-mindedly. "Is that you? What did you say?"

"Look out, there—"

BOOM!

The hedgehog and the blackbird rolled out of the bushes with laughter.

"Hey!" cried the hare indignantly. "There's nothing to laugh about. I could have broken something."

"Not a chance," said the hedgehog. "We've put these leaves down specially. We've been busy for *hours*. You fall softly."

"Yes, but still," said the hare, "it's dangerous!"

The hedgehog and the blackbird took no notice of him. They were busy putting the leaves back in a pile.

"Childish stuff," grumbled the hare.

"Come with me," said the owl. "They're not listening anyway."

The hare gave the leaves a kick and walked on with the owl. They had not gone far when they saw the wicked witch approaching. The witch was clearly in a bad mood. With an angry face she shuffled closer.

"Hello, witch," said the hare. "You'd better not go straight ahead. If you take this path here—"

"Move aside," snarled the witch. "I walk where I want."

"Yes, but," said the owl, "there, further on, there's—"

The witch pushed him aside and shuffled on.

The hare and the owl looked at each other and shrugged their shoulders.

"We've done our best," said the hare.

"She should've listened," said the owl.

BOOM!

For a moment it was very quiet in the wood.

Then there was a screeching noise: "Oohoo oohoo oohoo! Who did that? Come out!"

The hare and the owl heard fluttering and then the blackbird flew at full speed over their heads. The hedgehog came running as fast as he could. "Run!" he gasped, out of breath. "The witch! And she's hopping mad!"

"We don't need to run away," said the hare. "We haven't done anything."

The hedgehog had already gone.

It was just in time, because the wicked witch came charging along. The hare and the owl stepped aside to let her pass. But the witch stopped, put her hands on her hips, and asked threateningly, "Who tripped me?"

"Not us," said the owl. "We were just walking along here normally, you saw that yourself."

"Who did it then? Tell me!"

"I don't know," stammered the hare. "Do you know, owl?"

"No," said the owl. "Who could've done such a thing?"

"Most probably someone from outside the wood," said the hare.

"That's it," said the owl. "Someone from outside. No one from here would ever do that, never."

"Liars!" screamed the witch. "You know who it was, I can see!" She stamped her feet. "But it's up to you. You're coming with me until you tell me."

"But—but—but," stuttered the owl.

"That's not fair," said the hare.

"I don't care," cried the witch, stamping her feet again. "You are coming with me! Get going!"

The hedgehog sat at home and was eating a sandwich to calm himself down. He had just taken a bite when there was a loud banging on his door. He almost choked.

"The witch!" he piped, and crawled under the bed. The door opened and the blackbird came in.

"Hedgehog, are you at home?"

The hedgehog came out from under the bed. "Phew! I thought it was the witch."

"The witch has taken the hare and the owl with her!" cried the blackbird.

"What? What? Why?"

"Because they wouldn't say who had done it, you know, that rope. Without them noticing, I flew after them."

"How awful," said the hedgehog. "Do you want a sandwich?"

"This is no time to be eating sandwiches," said the blackbird sternly. "We've got to save our friends. Come with me."

"How are you going to do that?"

"We're going to tell the wicked witch that we tripped her. Then they'll be free again."

"But what about us?" groaned the hedge-hog. "The witch is furious! She'll turn us into something awful for certain or she'll lock us up!"

"Hmm," said the blackbird. "But we can't let the hare and the owl take the blame for something that *we* did."

The hedgehog looked down at the floor. "Surely the witch knows that they had nothing to do with it; she really won't do them any harm. But she will us. I'm not going."

The blackbird looked at him for a long time. "Then I'll go on my own," he said at last. He turned round and walked outside.

"Wait a minute, stop!" cried the hedgehog. "I'll go with you after all."

Silently they went on their way.

A short while later, they stood together in front of the witch's cottage.

"Will you knock?" whispered the blackbird. The hedgehog shook his head.

The blackbird took a deep breath and knocked softly on the door.

The door opened just a crack and the witch peered outside. "What do you want?"

"I . . . er . . . we," said the blackbird. "We've just come to say that we did it, we tripped you."

"Aha!" shrieked the witch. "Oohoo oohoo oohoo! I'll teach you to make a witch trip. Come inside."

With their heads bent, the blackbird and the hedgehog trudged inside the cottage.

BOOM! There they lay, flat on the floor in the room.

Shocked, the hare and the owl, who stood stirring a large pan, looked up.

The witch began to scream with laughter. "Hi hi, ha ha, ho ho! I brought your own rope here by magic! Hi hi, ha ha, ho ho!"

The hedgehog rubbed his leg. "Couldn't you have brought the leaves by magic?" he muttered.

The hare helped him get up.

"What has she done to you?" asked the hedgehog in a whisper.

"Nothing," said the owl. "We're helping her to make soup," and he pointed with a ladle at the pan on the fire.

The blackbird sniffed. "Mmm," he said approvingly.

The hedgehog looked at him angrily. "There, you see now, there's nothing to worry about. Just like you!"

The blackbird shrugged his shoulders. "I couldn't have known that. You know how nasty the witch can be. Oh, I mean . . ."

He looked round nervously. The witch had finally stopped laughing.

"That's that," she said. "That served you right. And I think I'll send you out of the wood for a while by magic; that'll teach you not to play these tricks."

"No, stop!" cried the hare. "You can't do that!"

"Oh no?" asked the witch. "And why not?"

"They made you trip—"

"Cowardly and wicked," screeched the witch.

"—but you did it too!"

"Oh yes," said the witch confused. "That's true. Then . . . er . . . well." She looked around helplessly.

The blackbird patted the hare on the shoulder. "How good of you not to tell on us."

"How good of you to come rescue us," said the hare.

"No problem," said the hedgehog. "We're friends, aren't we?"

The blackbird looked straight at him for a moment and cleared his throat. "That we are," he said.

The witch wiped her eyes, touched.

Ting! Ting! The owl was tapping the pan with the ladle. "The soup is ready!" He looked questioningly at the witch. "There's a lot of soup."

"Will you all stay for lunch?" asked the witch.

"Gladly!" said the hare and the owl and the blackbird.

The hedgehog was already sitting at the table.

A VISITOR

One morning, the hare thought: I wonder how the owl is getting on? I'll go and see if he's at home.

He had not walked far when he met the wicked witch.

"Good morning!" said the hare.

The witch looked at him searchingly.

"You look well," said the hare. "Been sitting in the sun?"

The witch mumbled something and went on.

Surprised, the hare watched her go. How very peculiar she was. What could be the matter? He shrugged his shoulders and walked slowly on.

"Hare!" he heard above his head. He looked up. It was the owl. "Hare! Wait a minute!" The owl swooped down and landed on the wood-path. "I'm glad you're here," he said. "I was just on my way to see you."

"And I was just on my way to see *you*," said the hare.

"I met the wicked witch this morning . . . ," the owl began.

"I just met her too!"

"Oh," said the owl. "And did you notice anything about her?"

"Yes, she behaved rather strangely. It was as

if she didn't recognize me."

"She didn't recognize me either!" cried the owl. "Could she be ill?"

"On the contrary, she looked very well," said the hare. "Even a little tanned."

"Tanned, yes. I noticed that too."

"Maybe she's been sitting in the sun too long."

"Or maybe she's lost her memory, that could—" The owl stopped and listened. "Someone's coming," he said. "Someone in a hurry."

The hedgehog came round the corner at full speed. "Out of the way!" he cried out of breath. "Oh, it's you." He dropped to the floor, puffing. "Phew . . ."

"What's the matter?" asked the hare.

"The witch . . . ," puffed the hedgehog. "She was after me . . . Phew . . . what a run!"

"Did she behave strangely?" asked the hare and the owl.

"Strangely? No, just like always, more's the pity."

"Did she recognize you?"

"Yes, of course she recognized me! Why else do you think I ran away so quickly?"

"Didn't you think that she looked different? Browner?"

"Of course not!" cried the hedgehog. "She was just like she always is. I told you that, didn't I!"

"She was different," said the owl.

"She was the same," said the hedgehog.

"Different!"

"The same!" The hedgehog got up. "You're blind," he said. "I'm going home. I'm far too frightened she'll be along again soon."

He headed off at a leisurely trot.

"Different," he grumbled. "Different and browner. What nonsense. As if I—" He stood stock-still. In front of him stood the wicked witch.

The hedgehog turned round as quick as lightning and started running back. But after a few paces he stopped again. In front of him stood the wicked witch!

Baffled, the hedgehog stared at her. The witch began to chuckle.

The hedgehog looked over his shoulder. There stood the witch chuckling as well. Quickly the hedgehog looked back again. There were two witches! One in front of him and one behind him.

"How can that be?" he whispered.

Both the witches roared with laughter at him. "My sister has come to visit," cried the wicked witch. "My sister from the south. It's great fun."

The hedgehog looked from the one to the other. Then he shot into the bushes. The witches

were laughing so much that they did not even notice.

The hedgehog raced back to the hare and the owl.

"The witch!" he cried. "I know why one is different and the other is the same. There are two of them! Her sister from the south is visiting."

"Her sister from the south," said the owl. "That's why she looked so tanned."

"Two witches . . ." The hare swallowed. "It could well become a very tense period . . ."

Now that the southern witch was there, the

animals had not a minute's peace anymore. If
they were on the run from one witch, they met
the other one. If one witch changed all the beetles so that they were as big as crows, the other
one changed all the crows so that they were as
small as beetles. If one of them made all the red
ants black, the other one made all the black ants
red. And if one witch was having a rest, the
other one was just getting going.

The animals did not dare go out. Frightened
and impatient, they waited until the southern
witch went home again. But the weeks passed
and she was still there.

◊◊◊

One evening the hare was going for a walk. It was getting dark; it was not so dangerous then. Something must be done, thought the hare. One witch, it is possible to live with that. But two . . . Pondering, he walked past the ferns.

Suddenly he heard a deep sigh.

"Oh dear," said the hare. "That's bound to be someone who's been bewitched."

But when he looked over the ferns, he dived back down immediately. It was the wicked witch.

Again the hare heard a deep sigh. Carefully

he looked again. The witch was sitting on an uprooted tree, her head bent, and she looked sad. The hare did not know what to do. I had better not interfere, he thought finally. The southern witch cannot be far off.

He began to walk away on tiptoe. But he had not gone two paces when he fell over a branch and there he lay, right in front of the witch. He held his breath.

The witch looked up and said gloomily, "Hello, hare."

"Hello," said the hare. He got up.

The witch sighed again.

"Is something the matter?" asked the hare shyly.

The witch nodded.

"What is it, then?"

"My sister," said the witch listlessly. "She's a good girl, but she interferes with everything. She always finds fault. I do everything wrong, she can do everything better. I can't stand it anymore."

"Well, I never," said the hare.

"She's so bossy," complained the witch. "Everything has to be done how she wants it and no other way. She acts as if it's her wood. I've had enough!"

"But she'll soon be going back home, won't she?"

"No!" said the witch. "That's just it. She

wants to stay here."

"Forever?" asked the hare, shocked.

"Forever," said the witch.

"There must be a way to make her go," said the hare. He sat down next to the witch. "If we . . . no, that's no good. We could perhaps . . . no, that would never work." Suddenly he jumped up. "I've got it!" he cried.

"Shh!" said the witch. "She'll hear you."

"I've got it," whispered the hare. "Listen . . ."

The next morning the wicked witch got up early. She took her suitcase out of the cupboard, put it on the middle of the table, and started packing.

The southern witch came right away to see what she was doing. "What are you doing?"

"I'm packing my suitcase."

"I can see that. But why?"

"I'm going away."

"Where are you going?"

The witch put a pile of clothes into the suitcase and said, "It's getting too busy for me here with all this witchcraft. And the wood is too small for two witches. I'm going south."

"South!"

"Yes," said the witch. "You want to stay here, so I can go to the south, can't I?"

"Certainly not!" shouted the southern witch. "I belong there, that's my territory, you've got no business there."

"But you want to stay here forever, don't you?"

"No! I'm going back! It's too busy for me here too. And too small. And too cold."

The wicked witch closed her suitcase with a bang. "I'm going to the south!"

"That's what you think!" cried the southern witch. "*I'm* going to the south!" She grabbed her broomstick and ran outside.

The hare and the owl and the hedgehog, who were hiding behind the witch's cottage, saw her flying above the wood, headed south.

"It worked!" they cried. "There she goes. Hooray!"

They ran to the front. The wicked witch stood beaming in the doorway.

"She has gone!" she cried. "Hare, your plan worked! She really thought that I wanted to go to the south!"

The hare and the hedgehog jumped up and down. "We've got rid of her! Hip, hip, hooray!"

"We're going to tell the others that they can come out again right away," said the owl.

"And that there's going to be a big party this evening," said the hare.

"Wait!" said the hedgehog. He frowned at the witch. "Are you going to put everything right again with your witchcraft?"

"It's already been done," said the witch.

The hedgehog sighed deeply. "What a relief that she's gone. One witch is more than enough."

The wicked witch looked straight at him and asked, "What do you mean?"

The hedgehog took a step back. "I mean . . . You're as good as two!"

The witch nodded, satisfied.

A WICKED PLAN

The wicked witch was sitting in front of her cottage in the sun. Her eyes were closed, but she was not asleep. The wicked witch was pondering.

It's time for something to happen again, she thought. I have not played any nasty tricks lately. It will not be long before no one is afraid of me. The witch heard something. She opened her eyes and saw the hedgehog sauntering closer. The hedgehog waved and said, "So, grandma, are you enjoying the sunshine?"

The witch winced. Grandma! Me! The wicked witch!

"Who do you think you are, impudent ruffian!" she snarled. But the hedgehog did not even hear her. Humming, he walked on. Furious, the witch watched him go.

Grandma! There you have it. They were not afraid of her anymore. But things were going to change. They would see some action in the wood.

Six rabbit children came running along, pushing and giggling. "Witch, witch, may we have a treat?"

The witch jumped up. "Off with you or I'll change you into pine cones!"

"Hi hi hi," giggled the rabbit children. "Pine cones. Silly witch," and playing, they went on.

Bewildered, the witch stared ahead. Those little ones were not even scared! The little ones thought it was a joke! When she used to say something like that, everyone flew off. This was going too far. Something had to be done.

"My very biggest pan," mumbled the witch. "My witch's cauldron. That's what I need." She walked over to a big iron cauldron that she had been using as a rain barrel for the last few months. Inch by inch, she shuffled with the heavy monster to the door. She was almost

there when the hare came running along.

"Be careful!" he cried. "Carrying such a heavy pan. Let me help. Where do you want it?"

The witch pointed inside.

"There we are," said the hare. "That's done. If you want to carry something heavy again, come and get me. You must be careful with your back at your age." And off he went into the wood.

"At your age," said the witch, furious. "I'll show them what I can still do at my age. Ha!"

She took her book of magic and began to glance through it.

What should she make? It had to be something terrible this time. Something that would remind everyone again that she was the boss, and always would be.

She read a page at the end of the book with interest. And then began to chuckle softly. Oohoo oohoo oohoo, how nasty that was! If she did that, she would have the animals in her power forever. That was what she would do. Just look and see what she needed for it. Aha, she had most of these things, but fresh herbs had to be picked as well. She got her basket and went on her way.

A short while later, she was rummaging near the sandbank.

"What are you doing? Looking for herbs? You're busy making a cough mixture, I expect," called the owl from a branch of a tree. "Shall I help you? Tell me what's needed."

"Black bennet root, stinking brome, bitter-weed and somnolent grass," said the witch.

"Leave it to me. Go home, and I'll come and bring them to you." The owl took the basket and set to work, whistling.

The wicked witch watched him with a wry smile. If only he knew, she thought.

◊◊◊

That afternoon, the hedgehog had a visit from the hare and the owl.

"We must have a word with you," said the hare. "About the witch. We're rather worried about her because she's old now and she is so isolated. This morning I was walking past and she was carrying a heavy pan. She can't possibly do that anymore, an old woman like that."

"The less she can do, the better," said the hedgehog softly. The hare looked at him reproachfully. The hedgehog blushed.

"We want to set up an emergency service," explained the owl. "If she needs help, then she can tell a bird and the bird can tell us. Are you going to join in?"

The hedgehog nodded. "Of course I'll join in."

"Then that's settled," said the hare. "We can get to work right away too, because when I put that pan inside for her this morning, I saw that her chair was badly broken. Shall we repair her chair as the first emergency service action and leave a bunch of flowers?"

"Wait a minute," said the hedgehog. "I've just baked a cake—we'll take that too."

The wicked witch was boiling her magic potion. A nasty smell spread through the rundown cottage. But the witch was not bothered by it.

"The worse it smells, the better it works," she muttered.

Now she still had to put viper-root and arrow-root poison in; then she would be ready.

She took her basket and went outside. But wherever she looked, the poisonous roots were nowhere to be found. I shall look elsewhere tomorrow, thought the witch at last. Tired, she shuffled back home.

But what was happening?

There was the hare with her witch's broom sweeping in front of the cottage. And behind the window, something was moving—there was someone inside as well!

"What's going on here?" screamed the witch.

The hare looked up. He was beaming. "We have a surprise. Come look," and he flung the cottage door open. The witch walked inside, amazed. Flowers were everywhere, her chair was well repaired, the owl and the hedgehog stood proudly next to the witch's cauldron and the witch's cauldron . . . was empty!

"The cauldron is empty!" cried the witch.

"Yes," said the hedgehog as he made a face. "We've thrown away your cough mixture because it smelled! It had probably gone bad."

The witch had to sit down for a minute. "You threw it away," she said flatly.

She clenched her fist and thought: Now

they've had it! I shall bewitch all three of them, here, right under their noses! But it was strange, she did not feel really angry . . .

The animals nudged one another. "She's touched," they whispered.

The hare cleared his throat and began to explain about the emergency service. "So now you know," he concluded, "we three are always ready to help you."

The witch did not know what to say. She rubbed her eyes and looked for her handkerchief. "I'll make tea," she said at last.

"We already have," said the owl.

"And cake," said the hedgehog.

"Witch, witch," cried the rabbit voices outside. "Witch, may we have a treat?"

"Give those little ones a piece of cake too," said the witch. "Come in, all of you!"

It had begun to grow dark when the animals finally went on their way. The witch stood in the doorway and waved after them.

"Bye, dear witch, bye!" cried the rabbit children as long as they could see her.

The witch went inside. Dear witch! She still had to get used to it. She took her book of magic. She glanced through it slowly and then closed it with a bang. She walked with it to the cupboard and tucked it way in the back.

"I won't be needing it again for some time,"

said the witch.

For a moment, she stood undecided in front of the cupboard. Then she pulled the book a little bit forward again.

"You never know," she mumbled.

Contented, she sat in her chair and ate the last piece of cake.

Hanna Kraan was born in 1946 in Rotterdam, where she still lives, teaching Italian and working as an interpreter. She has been writing short stories for children since 1973. *Tales of the Wicked Witch* is her first full-length book.

Elisabeth Koolschijn was born in Rhiwbina, Wales. After moving to the Netherlands, she taught at the English school in The Hague.